THE BYGONE BOYFRIEND

A SHORT STORY

ALEXANDRIA BLAELOCK

BlueMere Books
MELBOURNE, AUSTRALIA

For permission requests, please contact
enquiries@bluemerebooks.com.

Ordering Information:
Discounts are available on quantity purchases. For details, contact orders@bluemerebooks.com.

The Bygone Boyfriend/Alexandria Blaelock
paperback ISBN: 978-1-925749-43-4
digital ISBN: 978-1-925749-44-1

Book Layout © BookDesignTemplates.com

THE BYGONE BOYFRIEND

Jennifer strolled down Perth's main street. When she was younger, the City had seemed so big and so busy.

But having lived in cities ten or more times the size, across Europe, Asia and America, now it just seemed quaint.

So small and slow it barely moved at all.

A cute holiday town - great to visit, but not to live.

Like a beach holiday, without the beach.

Or getting off the train while it was still moving.

She struggled to summon up a feeling of attachment to the city she'd grown up in.

The one most would define as her home town, even though she'd chosen not to return.

Hadn't intended ever to come back.

The late afternoon sunshine was warm against her back, too warm in fact, though that was to be expected given it was Summer.

The golden Summer sun was about the only thing that felt the same as she remembered.

Though it rarely rains when you remember your childhood does it?

The city's sights, sounds and smells were all wrong, it wasn't like home at all.

The ghosts of past friends, jobs, and dates swirling around her didn't help at all.

The café where she'd bought her first cappuccino was now a cut-price makeup outlet.

The movie theatre where she'd fallen in love with Monty Python while watching *Life of Brian* was a lap dancing club.

Not even her old office building had escaped unscathed.

It was now a discounted hotel, and she'd come within a hair's breadth of trying to book a room where her desk used to be.

Only the corporate travel policy and prospects for reimbursement prevented it.

The travel agent she'd bought her one-way ticket out of this hell hole was a lingerie shop. Selling a better class of lingerie than had been available before she'd left.

And possibly worst of all, her Friday night drinking hole, where you could spin the wheel and win a hot roasted chicken for a late-night drunken snack, was now an underground car park.

Tired of walking, she stopped at an open-air bar in the mall.

When she'd left, it had been a four-lane street jam-packed with traffic, two traffic lights away from the train station. Now it was an open space on top of a recently constructed underground station.

She pushed her way through the tourists, and took a seat at a table, resting her bag on the seat next to her.

Large trees grew from holes in the paving. They weren't particularly tall yet, only just reaching the second story of the surrounding buildings, but they shaded the pedestrians milling beneath them well enough.

She admired the way the City had invested in redevelopment in line with the vision of a prosperous and popular international city.

If you build it, and all that, though they still had a way to go.

Or was she witnessing the pivot between thriving metropolis and ghost town?

A slight exhaust scented breeze fanned the leaves and cooled her face.

She leaned back in her seat and hooked a foot around the seat opposite to pull it closer.

Then kicked off her sandals, put her bare feet on the chair, and her hands behind the back of her neck.

The breeze blew through the loose weave of her shirt, evaporating the sweat from her body.

The place couldn't have been more alien if it was a city she'd never visited before.

Though technically, this City wasn't the one she'd left, but the one that had replaced it.

She'd only been away for 15 years, but she had an idea of how Rip Van Winkle might have felt when he woke up.

Everything was the same, only different. Where there'd once been a feeling of love, there was now revulsion.

It felt like the City was judging her, and unlike her dog, it didn't forgive her long absence.

Though time must move differently for dogs than Cities.

When a waitress in a long black apron arrived, she ordered Campari and soda, and a bowl of marinated olives.

Despite the City's rejection, it was sort of nice to be alone, unknown and unnoticed in the crowd.

To have some quiet space away from her worries, both here and at home.

She sighed, and stretched, pushing her toes toward the back of the chair, and opening her arms further behind her neck.

Then she took her black straw hat off, put it on top of her bag and ruffled her hair.

The stiffening breeze was pleasant against her sweaty scalp.

Her bag pinged, and she pulled her phone out to see what her assistant wanted.

No changes to the presentation, good luck tomorrow, make time to have some fun.

Excellent news; time contingency not required, and she had the night off.

Her drink arrived, and she drank half of it before the ice could melt and water it down. Then went back to watching the people.

Even though she knew it was unlikely she'd see anyone familiar, she couldn't help looking for familiar faces in the steady stream of people leaving the City as quickly as possible.

She wondered what her old friends might be like. Would they reject her as completely as the City had? Had she grown beyond them too?

She closed her eyes and tried to imagine what calling her one-time best friend might be like.

Though she'd have to make a few phone calls to get Amy's number.

Might be a bit of a conversation required to get it too, Amy's mother had never liked her much.

Come to think of it, most of her friend's mothers hadn't liked her much either.

Was that because of something she'd done, or because her Dad was the town drunk?

She'd never know for sure, though it stood to reason they thought she was a "bad" girl and a "bad" influence. Still not entirely sure what that was.

She hadn't given it much thought at the time, aside from thinking it was funny.

Anyway, there was really only Jason she wouldn't mind seeing again.

Though the prospect was terrifying.

She'd loved him to the peak of embarrassing obsession, and treated him so badly at the end.

Then again, he'd cheated on her with Helen back then, so wasn't her fury justified?

Though in retrospect, she appreciated his bluntness. He'd given her what she'd needed to make a clean break, move away and forge a new life for herself.

Ridiculously, of all the things she'd done and not done, she regretted not sleeping with him the most.

And if she stumbled across a time machine, she'd be tempted to haul the chrononaut out and take a trip back to fix that.

She snorted at the idea.

Poor innocent Jason wouldn't know what hit him - some old to him woman cracking on to him and not taking the hint when he politely asked her to leave him alone.

Just as well you can't go back, only go forward. Some things are better left in the past where they belong.

And this time tomorrow, she'd be on her way back home to her normal life, leaving Jason and this town behind her, in the past where they belonged.

But what was she afraid of?

That the town knew who she really was, and wasn't fooled by the veneer of confidence she showed to the world?

That it saw her for the damaged little girl she had been, not the competent woman she'd become.

And as for Jason, did she think after all this time she'd lose control of herself and beg him to take her back?

Or was she more afraid she'd not be able to resist him should he call her back?

One thing for sure, there were way too many memories in this town, and the sooner she left them behind, the better.

If they won the bid, someone else could take over the negotiations.

《《 • 》》

Jason wouldn't have noticed her if she hadn't suddenly leant over to check her phone as he was walking along the balcony above her.

And even then, he might not have noticed her at all if she hadn't seemed so brisk, efficient and stunningly well-groomed in comparison to the drooping, ill-dressed tourists sitting in Garibaldi's Bar.

Located just about where exhaustion hit, Garibaldi's was a bit of a tourist trap. And as usual, it was full of grubby limp t-shirts.

Except for the woman in the crisp white linen shirt, and black straw hat.

There was something about her that pulled at the edge of his memory like a hangnail.

Despite himself, he paused, leaning on the balustrade to watch her, trying to figure it out so he could forget about her and focus on to his blind date.

She took her hat off, tilting her head back to reveal dark red coloured lips and ruffling her short hair with matching red nail polish tipped fingers.

There was an economy about her movements, an angular fluidity as if she was the living embodiment of the linen she was wearing.

She took up space, looking like the kind of independent woman who's more accustomed to giving orders than taking them.

It was a little bit sexy.

Then he caught a glimpse of her face between the leaves and realised who she was.

Jennifer Hughes.

His first love, Jennifer Hughes.

The girl he'd foolishly dumped for another, who'd dumped him not long after.

Jennifer, who wasn't wearing any rings!

He'd hurt her feelings so deeply he was ashamed to go back to her and ask her forgivingness.

She'd moved away, and so far as he knew, had never been back.

Blind date forgotten, he turned and headed back towards the stairs. He had to get down there and make contact before he lost her again.

He walked up and down beside the bar a few times, hoping she'd see him and call out to him, or maybe leave so he could run into her.

No such luck.

Maybe she didn't recognise him.

He walked towards a shop window and assessed his reflection, then smoothed back his hair.

A girl inside started laughing, and he quickly turned away, assuming she was laughing at him.

Then, pausing to take a deep breath, he plunged into the bar before he could change his mind.

《《 • 》》

"Jennifer?" a male voice asked.

The sound of her name startled her, but she didn't believe he was talking to her, so she didn't open her eyes and tried to ignore the voice.

Clearly, it was some other Jennifer.

"Jennifer Hughes, is that you?"

No doubting it now, he was talking to her.

She opened her eyes and looked up into a vaguely familiar face.

"It's me, Jason Spencer."

She looked more closely, and yes; it probably was him.

What was it Mum used to say, think of the devil and he's sure to appear?

Looks like she was right about that after all.

Jennifer hoped the wind didn't change then, the look on her face was probably not the most attractive in her arsenal.

Campari on an empty stomach got in her way as she struggled to get her feet back on the ground and sit upright.

He was older, naturally, more relaxed in his body and confident about himself.

His snug t-shirt and well-fitted jeans didn't hide the fact his weedy body had filled out with muscle, the kind of muscle that hinted at hard work rather than hours in the gym.

His blazer suggested he was headed to a date, and she felt a flash of jealousy.

Jason Spencer wasn't a boy any more, he'd become a man and a fine-looking man at that.

"Ah, hello, Jason. Long-time no see," and she winced.

Oh God, had she really said those stupid words?

He smiled, and sat down uninvited, "you look just the same."

"God I hope not. I hope I look like I know what I'm doing now."

He laughed, his one-time wind chime giggle, now deepened to a chuckle.

He gestured to attract the waitress' attention, "Heineken please," and pointing at her glass, "and another of those."

The waitress smiled and nodded, much friendlier towards him than Jennifer.

"Well, looks like you've still got it," she said, slightly miffed.

He snorted, "Not as much as you might think, I'm old and irrelevant now."

"I think I might know that feeling better than you."

He snorted again.

"How's Helen?" Jennifer asked, needing to get that out of the way first.

"Who?"

"Helen. You must remember Helen."

"Oh, yeah. Helen. We broke up years ago. I'm surprised you remember her."

Oops, Jennifer thought.

"So, how's it going?" he asked.

She guessed that was code for "are you single," but she was here for one night only.

She wouldn't mind fucking him out of curiosity, but it couldn't be any more than that.

Unless he was very good and then she might stretch to twice before she went home.

Anything more than that was a recipe for disaster.

But as he smiled at her, she had the idea he might be interested in a night or more with her.

"Fine," she took a gulp of her drink, "busy. You?"

She looked at her watch to emphasise how busy she was, but he laughed, and she rested her wrist on the table.

He covered her hand with his, gently stroking the back of her hand with his thumb.

She noticed he wasn't wearing any rings.

Not that it meant much, but, he wasn't wearing any rings.

"I don't think you're busy. And I have an idea you're not fine too."

She went still, watching him smile at her, feeling the exquisite torture of his soft touch.

It felt like he was staking a claim.

Realising she was losing the battle, she tried to pull her hand back, but he tightened his grip slightly, and after a couple of tugs, she let him keep it.

She opened her mouth to deny it, but on a purely objective level, it was the truth.

She wasn't fine or busy.

"How's your mother?" she asked, trying to turn the conversation in a different direction.

"The same. If you have time, I'm sure she'd love to see you."

Jennifer smiled, Mrs Spencer was the only mother she'd known who'd seemed to see her, not her family.

"I wish I could, but I'm leaving tomorrow."

The waitress arrived with their drinks, bumping Jennifer.

Waking her up.

"Thank you," said Jason, releasing her hand and reaching for his drink.

"Thank you," Jennifer said simultaneously, and the waitress smiled and nodded in acknowledgement as Jason shouted, "Jinx! Now you have to grant me a wish."

She grimaced and drained the last of her first drink.

"What's your wish then?"

"Have dinner with me."

Jinx or not, she knew she ought to say no, and took a sip of her fresh drink to stall.

"Say you'll have dinner with me."

One and a bit cocktails with half a bowl of olives aren't the best foundation for rational decision making.

And it would be nice to spend an evening sitting at a table, eating with a person, not cross-legged on the couch eating with the dog.

There would be plenty more of those evenings when she got back home.

She looked at her watch again, and he quirked an eyebrow at her.

Why was she supposed to be avoiding him again?

"I'll have dinner with you."

His face lit up, and he was so dazzling she couldn't change her mind.

Or tell him she only said it because he told her to.

《《 • 》》

She said yes!

Well not technically yes, but at least she didn't say no.

He knew he was grinning like a lunatic, and took a swig of beer to cover it.

Then his phone rang.

Shit! The blind date.

She settled more comfortably into her seat, picked up her drink, and rested it on her lip with an air of resignation he didn't much like.

He couldn't afford to give her any time to change her mind.

So, he pulled his phone from his jacket, turned it off without looking at it, and slipped it back in his pocket.

He grinned again at her surprise.

If she was leaving tomorrow, the stakes were high, and he had to do something to intrigue her. Something to keep her interested and her attention focused on him.

Could he gamify the evening?

"If I dared you, would you turn your phone off too?"

She snorted, "there's no need to dare me, there's no one I'd answer right now."

She pulled her phone from her bag and turned it off.

No one she wanted to talk to!

"It's kind of old fashioned isn't it, not stressing about the phone ringing?"

"Speak for yourself," she said. "My sister and I always raced each other to get to the phone first, though it was more often for her than for me."

"Well, we had walkie-talkies, remember?"

She snorted. "Oh yeah.

"Talking to each other in bed seemed very naughty, didn't it? I was terrified my mother would find out."

He fist-pumped inside, he'd got her thoughts into bed with him, even if they were only 12 at the time.

She softened a little into her chair as if thinking about the age before everything started to get more complicated was relaxing.

Though compared to all the complications of being an adult, maybe it was.

He tilted his beer bottle and started peeling the label off, "those were the days, weren't they?"

"I dunno, so much has happened since then. That girl seems as much a stranger to me as the City does right now."

The ice in her glass clinked, and a drip of condensation fell in her lap.

"Do you sometimes wish you were still a child?" he asked.

"God no. When you're a girl, there's always someone telling you what to do and how to behave."

He laughed.

"Kind of like stop running, or shouting, or tracking dirt through the house?"

"More like pull your skirt down, why don't you smile, why can't you act more like a lady."

"I never noticed."

"How could you? You only had brothers."

They fell silent for a moment while he struggled to understand childhood from a girl's perspective.

"I don't seem to recall you being very ladylike."

"Exactly," she laughed. "Not much has changed since then."

He leaned towards her, "I think I like this version of you. You're sort of more substantial."

"Substantial? I'm not sure that's a compliment."

He leaned his elbows on the table as he leaned closer.

"When you were a kid, you had a knack of disappearing into the background, almost as if you turned sideways and disappeared."

She laughed a little, "you learn to disappear when you live in a house full of drunken violence. That's why I liked your place, it always felt safe."

"I can't even imagine what that must have been like."

She put her drink down and patted his hand, "you're the lucky one then."

He captured her hand as she pulled away and kissed the back of it, "I'm sorry you had to go through that."

"What doesn't kill you makes you stronger hey?

Anyway, those experiences made me who I am today. I'm afraid to think who I might have become if things had been any different."

He swallowed his thickening throat. Who would she have become if he hadn't been blinded by Helen?

"I'm starving," she said, "what were you thinking for dinner."

It didn't matter, as long as it wasn't anywhere near where his blind date was waiting. Should it be somewhere she hadn't been, or somewhere they'd used to go together?

"Do you remember the food court we used to buy lunch when we came into town to go to the pictures?"

She smiled, "what was it? Golden Palace? Dragon Inn?"

"Doesn't matter, that dive's gone now, but there's an excellent Japanese restaurant there now. Give it a try?"

"Sure," she said, gulping her drink and collecting her bag and hat, "let's go."

《《 • 》》

Jennifer was still lost in a haze of childhood memories. Building dams with Jason, playing hide and seek with Jason, comparing naked boy and girl bits with Jason.

In retrospect, they were lucky no one had found their cubby house. That's one of the benefits of living on the outskirts of a city she supposed.

They'd been so much a part of each other's lives until their late teens. From this great distance, it was amazing she'd let someone else come between them. That she hadn't sent him away to Helen with her best wishes but kept in touch.

Or had that been more to do with Helen?

As they walked, she started thinking about the next day as a different kind of next day.

This thing between them didn't have to be a start, it could be an end instead.

She could take him back to her reasonably priced, reasonably central hotel and do that thing she'd been regretting.

It might have been the Campari talking, but why not get him out of her system, get some psychobabble closure, and go home the next day with no regrets.

So when he took her hand, she laced her fingers through his and told herself it didn't matter that their hands still fit perfectly.

Despite having lived in Tokyo for several years, she let him order the food.

She sat on one hip on her cushion, leaning towards him, legs to the other side.

Maybe a little closer than necessary, but he didn't seem to mind.

It seemed the time for talking was done for the moment, as they focused on the food.

He was right, it was delicious, as well as beautifully prepared and arranged as Japanese food always is.

She placed a little eel on his rice to try, and he put a little chicken on hers. And laughed when he duelled with her chopsticks for a share of the seaweed salad.

He filled her Saki cup, and after taking a sip, she offered it back to him. He held her eyes as he drained the cup, then refilled it and handed it back.

Now and again, she let her hand brush his, or leaned against him.

He nudged her shoulder with his or patted her thigh.

And as the meal came to an end, and he started stacking up the dishes, she was filled with affection for him.

He was the first person she could remember outside of her family.

And now they were sitting together, as comfortably as if they'd never been apart.

All of a sudden, she understood.

Whether they'd been together or not, he'd always been the bedrock of her life.

The only person she'd ever pushed back against, was him.

《《 • 》》

Jason was focused on stacking the dishes back the way they'd arrived when he realised Jennifer had gone still.

He wasn't afraid exactly, but sensed the change meant something, so he looked at her just as she reached across to kiss him.

Just a little peck, presumably meant for his cheek.

But it was enough for him.

He left the dishes where they were and reached out one hand to cup her jaw, watching for some sign of rejection.

He saw none and slowly leaned towards her to kiss her lips.

So slowly, it seemed she got impatient and leaned towards him, grabbing his face in both hands and kissing his lips.

She'd done the same thing for their first proper kiss, which was just as well because he'd been almost as scared then as he was now.

What if he was doing it wrong, what if she didn't like it, what if she left him.

But this time, she was the one who wanted her independence - how many times had she said she was leaving?

You couldn't fault her for warning him, but it made him wonder.

What was he willing to put on the line to keep her? Could he risk everything the way she had back then?

She broke off the kiss and dropped her hands.

He looked at her for a while, looking for some sign of what she was thinking.

Could he let the dice fall, knowing they were loaded in her favour?

Knowing he was going to lose her, and knowing if he wanted her, he'd have to chase her?

Could he live with himself if he let this opportunity pass?

No.

He couldn't.

"Shall we get out of here?"

《《 • 》》

Back at her disappointingly unsexy hotel room, Jennifer tried not to let her nerves get in the way.

She wasn't a teenager anymore, and should he care to, Jason could read her life's history mapped in the scars on her body.

Out of defiance, she left the lights on as he peeled back her clothing to reveal her practical underwear and the first of her surgical scars.

He winced but didn't say anything, only kissed each one as he uncovered it.

Perhaps he could see past it, through the girl she had been to the woman she was today.

Not that it mattered, she still couldn't stay.

But she started to wonder whether there was a Jason shaped space in her life.

She'd gone too far from her life here, and she had too much to lose.

She couldn't let it all go to come back to him now.

She shrugged her thoughts away, and for the next few hours, focused on the sensations he roused in her body.

And after a point, fell asleep in his arms.

She woke early the next morning and left him sleeping while she took a shower and dressed.

As she did her makeup, she watched him in the mirror for a while, trying to decide whether he was really asleep or just pretending because he didn't know what to say to her.

But given his masterful performance, there was no need for him to be embarrassed, and he probably deserved his rest.

She quietly packed her carry-on bag and wheeled it to the door. And then she picked his clothes off the floor and folded them on the chair.

It was too late now, but she wished she'd woken him up for another round before she left.

All that was left was to decide whether she wanted to see him again or not.

And she'd probably be less upset to see him again than not, so what to do?

A long time ago he'd cheated on her, and he'd given her a blunt assessment of her future potential with him.

That was, nil.

Though, if the last night had been any indication, he might have changed his mind.

And if he had, then he should pursue her.

If he didn't, then she'd know it was over.

She'd let him choose.

Smiling, she stood at the hotel desk and pulled out some paper and an envelope. She wrote a small note.

Had fun, call if you dare.
 *J*

She folded the note into the envelope and put it on top of his clothes where he was unlikely to miss it.

It had been fun, and it would be interesting to see what came next.

THE END

ABOUT THE AUTHOR

Alexandria Blaelock writes stories, some of them for *Ellery Queen's Mystery Magazine* and *Pulphouse Fiction Magazine*. She's also written four self-help books applying business techniques to personal matters like getting dressed, cleaning house, and feeding your friends.

As a recovering Project Manager, she's probably too fond of sticking to plan. She lives in a forest because she enjoys birdsong, the scent of gum leaves and the sun on her face. When not telecommuting to parallel universes from her Melbourne based imagination, she watches K-dramas, talks to animals, and drinks Campari.
At the same time.

Discover more at www.alexandriablaelock.com.

OTHER SHORT STORIES BY ALEXANDRIA BLAELOCK

Alma's Grace
Balancing the Book
Bygone Boyfriend
Carmelita Basingstoke
Fate in Your Hands
Kiss of Death
Lady of the Looking Glass
Life in the Security Directorate
Long Weekend in the Snow
Love in the Security Directorate
Morning Star, Evening Star, Superstar
Needy Bitch
Payton's Run
Phoenix Child
Secret Singer
Shining Star
Ship in a Bottle
Simone Says Hands in the Air
The Day the Schedule Broke
The Guardian's Vigil
Toy Soldiers

BOOKS BY ALEXANDRIA BLAELOCK

FICTION

That Love Nonsense

MS BLAELOCK'S BOOKS

Stress Free Dinner Parties
Signature Wardrobe Planning
Holistic Personal Finance
Minimally Viable Housekeeping